The Key

A Taylor and Alan Adventure

Jackie Mae

and

Alison Taylor

Illustrated by
James Khoui

Edited by
Ashton Farmanara

Compiled by
Carolyn Sheltraw

ISBN: 978-0-9916149-6-7 (paperback)
978-0-9916149-7-4 (ebook)

Printed in the United States of America

Other books by Jackie Mae:

The Ones

A Lifetime to Wait

~

Other books in

A Taylor and Alan Adventure:

Twilight of Doom

To,

My husband, always my knight

And a special thanks to,

Lu Ann Marshall whose stories and tour
inspired me

And to,

My grandchildren,
Whose enduring love has made a difference
in our lives

And to,

Billy “Box Turtle” Heinbuch
With Girl Scouts of Central Maryland’s
Caitlin Dunbar Nature Center
For sharing his passion and knowledge

"Our ecosystem is tied to our future,"
A portion of the proceeds from the sale of this book will go to
The Caitlin Dunbar Nature Center.

Jackie Mae

A Note from Jackie Mae:

Welcome. With our ever-depleting habitats, the disappearance of the forests along with their closely held secrets, and the potential rise of the oceans, there seem to be a lot of uncertainty. Our children are our hope for the future; they should be respected and valued for the gifts they bring. With love and guidance, raising respectful and mindful children, I know we can all say with certainty the place we call home will be a better place.

Table of Contents

Chapter One

One day past the summer fields, over the hills, beyond the highway and overhang, below the sky-scraper, and through the mall was the theater to end all theaters.

Taylor and Alan had waited so long for the opening. Today was the day—they had it all planned out. They would do their chores first thing after they had breakfast while rushing their parents along. Hopefully they would be at the mall by noontime. That would leave them plenty of time to do a little shopping and eat at that awesome restaurant, Joe's Pick, which served pizza with the yummy, thick, cheese-stuffed crust. It was sooo gooey it practically melted in your mouth. From there it was all mapped out—they would head on over to the brand new theater, called Big John's Mall 9.

Taylor and Alan had been forced to endure trailers of their favorite sequel for months now. It was so difficult waiting for the movie to arrive. They had seen the trailer a million times by now. The movie, titled "The Mushroom Had a Top," was sort of weird, but this was the third in the series and all their classmates, including Taylor and Alan, had seen the previous two movies at least twice. This sequel was thought to be the best one yet. Anticipation was high and Taylor and Alan had begged their parents to take them on opening day as a special treat.

Taylor had saved up over $30.00, promising to help pay for everyone. She had done chores, watched Mrs. Henderson's cat on several occasions, and had maintained good grades, even improving on last semester's grades.

Alan had pretty much done the same, doing his chores, mowing the neighbor's grass, and carrying

Mr. Ford's groceries in from the car every Saturday morning. Mr. Ford had been in, what their mother had described as, "the recent conflict," and had lost his left leg to a roadside bomb. Mr. Ford was a really nice man and although he didn't really need Alan's help, Alan enjoyed spending time with him.

They left by 11:45 a.m., which was ahead of schedule, with Taylor and Alan smiling at each other as they pulled into the mall parking garage. They were on level 4 so all they had to do was take the sky walkway directly into the theater entrance. It was still early so not too many people had arrived yet. That had been Taylor and Alan's plan all along—to get there early and catch the movie before the prices went up for the evening showings.

"Okay kids, let's go down to Brown's ShoeTown real quick, so I can dart in and out. I want to see if they have a size 10 in my favorite shoe," announced Dad. Dad didn't come to the mall much and his favorite Brown shoe now had a slight hole in the sole.

"Fine," said Mom. "I will take both the kids with me to purchase the tickets. I'll meet you at Brown's as soon as we are done."

They headed over to the ticket booth where the poster of the movie caught Taylor's eye. And so it all began…

"I love that," I exclaimed. "Look at the mushroom, Alan!"

There was awe in my voice. The poster was approximately 10 feet high by about 4 feet wide. It was humongous. It was way taller than I was. It depicted a large mushroom with the members of the rebellion defending it against the invaders. Of course, the mushroom was really a distant planet that earthlings had started a new colony on.

I loved the character, Arianna, because she was strong. She had superb intellect, meaning she could think fast on her feet, and she worked out every day with another strong character, Dirk. Together they led the rebellion against the invading Smashers, a group of bad guys from a neighboring galaxy, planet MAB497.

Alan looked over the poster. “Yeah, doesn’t that look cool?”

Alan loved anything having to do with a battle. I, however, loved more of a plot to the story. This was a classic good vs. bad movie, with the very best in special effects, something I never got tired of.

I was in somewhat of a daze, standing there in front of the poster, daydreaming about what the movie might be about, imagining all the possible endings that this sequel might have. I imagined how I would have ended the movie if I had written the movie script. Movie script was a fancy term for the story. I had learned that term from Lucy, a student in my 3rd period math class. Her dad was a big time movie writer, or so Lucy said. Personally, I wasn’t so sure because I had never heard of Lucy’s dad.

“Jeez, Taylor—where are you?” hollered Alan. “C’mon.”

I hurried to stand beside them in line. “Excuse me,” I was forced to say three times to get by several kids who looked at me like I might be butting in line. I quickly started talking to Alan, questioning him if he thought the movie would be a good one, so everyone knew I wasn't butting in line, but rather, just trying to get to my family.

We bought the tickets and headed down the escalator in the direction of Brown's ShoeTown when I spotted the gadget store. Actually, it was a store with furniture in it but it also had the coolest gadgets all in one store that Taylor had ever seen. There were gadgets for the refrigerator, the grill, your bedroom desk, even the bathroom. I loved taking my time, discovering a new gadget we needed each time I went in there.

"Mom, can I look in here for a little while? Please?" I asked.

Mom stood in front of the store looking at me. "Sure, Brown's is just next door. Alan you have to stay right beside your sister, okay? I will just let Dad know we bought the tickets and then I will come right back over."

"Sure," said Alan. I think Alan didn't complain

because, he too, wanted to look over all the cool gadgets. We didn't really come very often and there was bound to be something new and exciting.

We moved into the store looking over a table of gadgcts that were for every well-organized kid's bedroom. I saw the clip first. It was a clip that came in several colors, to hold just about anything. It was oversized, about the size of my fist, probably plastic, and it had a magnet on the backside.

I could certainly use one of those I thought. It could go on my metal cabinet, the one I got from Aunt Myrtle when she was going to trash it because it didn't fit into her design anymore, or maybe I could use it to hold my hair scrunches in the netting I had hanging in front of my mirror. There were a million uses for this handy gadget.

"I'm going to ask mom if I can get one of these with the money I have saved up," I told Alan.

"Yeah, that's a really useful gadget. I think I will get one too," added Alan.

By the time mom and dad had arrived, we had moved on to other gadgets that were way cooler, and had all but forgotten about the clip.

I saw a portable checkers set. I almost went past it but the design on the knapsack caught my eye. It was made of canvas and linen. It had small, flat, lightweight wooden pieces. The cloth board folded in on itself and became a knapsack that you could actually use to carry small items in. It was way cool. It was the perfect thing to take around the neighborhood with me. My friends and I loved playing checkers. The price was $16.99 but they were having a blow-out one day only sale for 75% off.

Mom said I could purchase it because I was actually going to be doing something with my mind. Parents always need to rationalize things, because us kids, well most of us kids, are more live-in-the-moment kind of kids.

"Let's go kids," announced Dad. He was carrying a Brown's ShoeTown bag so I supposed he must have gotten a new pair of shoes. "I see a line forming over at the restaurant you guys asked to go to. We will have to hurry up a little bit or we just might be late for the show."

That got my attention. No matter what, I didn't want to be late for our movie. We headed for the restaurant and got in line. After standing there for several minutes I started to worry that we would have to pick another restaurant when the hostess called our name. She escorted us to a large booth that was decorated like something out of a rainforest.

Alan and I liked this restaurant for their specialty pizzas, but the décor was an added bonus, as far as I was concerned. The whole restaurant looked like a rainforest, hanging vines lined all the lighting fixtures, sounds of the rainforest were heard throughout, and there was even a huge tank in the middle of the restaurant where people could walk around it to see all the creatures staring back at you. Written on the table and seats themselves were trivia questions about the rainforest that Alan and I were pretty good at answering.

Mom read one question and asked Alan to answer it. It was such an easy question, I almost blurted out the answer. She asked, “What are the two major types of rainforest?

By the expression on Alan’s face, smiling from ear to ear, he thought it was an easy question too. “That would be the temperate and tropical rainforests. Boom!” answered Alan.

“Very good Alan,” replied Mom. I could see her looking around for a good question to ask me.

She had found one. “Your turn Taylor.” Mom looked over at me.

“Bet you can’t find one I can’t answer,” I said smugly.

“Oh really, you’re on missy,” said Mom. She looked around for a harder question. Maybe I shouldn’t have said anything—too late now. She found one.

Mom asked her question. “How much of the earth’s surface is covered by the rainforest: a. <2% b. 10% or c. 12% ?”

Mom sure did need to find harder questions now that we were getting older. "Sorry Mom, too easy. The answer is less than 2 percent."

Mom said, "You are correct. It seems I will have to revise my questions for next time."

The pizza arrived. I dug right into my slice of pizza. It was like heaven. The gooey cheesy-stuffed crust was making my taste buds sing. Dad had ordered some yummy bread sticks with marinara dipping sauce, my favorite. This was turning out to be the best day ever. I was taking my last sip of soda when Dad spoke.

"Okay, let's get going."

Chapter Two

I didn't want to be late. That was for sure. I wanted to get there early, so we could find the very best seats—that part was crucial to the whole plan—and then have enough time to get snacks or maybe someone would need a last minute bathroom break.

It never failed that when we went to the movies someone would need to go to the restroom after the beginning remarks. You know, right as the beginning of the movie was taking place, one of the most important parts. You had to watch the beginning or else you wouldn't understand what was going on. Then the whispering would begin, "I'll take this kid and I'll stay here with the other," kind of stuff.

Of course this past year I turned a year older and was now allowed to go with Alan to the concession stand and back without one of my parents. Mom was pretty strict about things like that.

Mom handed the ticket taker our tickets and then gave each one of us the ticket stub to put in our pockets just in case we needed to prove we bought tickets for the movie.

As we entered the theater, I mapped out in my mind the exact locations of the bathrooms, just in case I needed to go, so I could be in and out in a hurry. I didn't want to miss one second of the movie.

This was going to be the greatest movie experience ever Alan had told me. Saeed and Peter, two of Alan's friends, told Alan about how some of the stunts in the movie were made. Alan said they knew all about stuff like that.

We entered the doors leading to the brand new theater seats. These seats were oversized, plush with lots of comfy material for your bottom, along with a headrest. The seats even reclined a tiny bit and had drink holders and a slide-out tray so you could put your popcorn or candy down. The aisles were larger than the regular theater aisles and the space between each row of seats was much larger than I remembered seeing at any other theater I had been to. Positive I wouldn't have to sweep my legs to the side so people could get by, I was already very happy.

Dad and Alan debated over the best row and seat selection, which was a huge deal in our family because your seat determined how fast you could get in and out of your seat, how fast you could go the bathroom and back, where you could see and hear the best, and where the air-conditioning would be hitting Dad. Dad was always hot it seemed and he liked to feel nice and cool at the movies. Mom carried a small sweater with her every time we went to the movies, even in the summertime. She was always cold in the theater. Mom and Dad had discussions about the air-conditioning in the car too, but that's a whole other story.

After settling down, finally, in the very best seat, I started looking around me. Each row of seats were well spaced out so if someone sat in front of you that was tall, and maybe wore a hat they forgot to politely take off, you could still see the screen without missing any part of it.

And it smelled good in here unlike some theaters that had a musky smell, some had a downright bad smell that was made worse by putting too much air freshener on top of it. But this theater was brand new so not much soda or candy had been dropped on the carpet yet. I shuddered at the thought of all those lurking, dirty germs. Hopefully they had a good cleaning crew at this theater.

But no time to think those negative thoughts, I told myself. *I'm at Big John's Mall 9, and I will only think good thoughts. No sense ruining any part of the whole experience.* I asked Mom when the movie would start.

"We are twenty-five minutes early Taylor," answered Mom. "Remember how important it is to get the right seat. Now we have enough time to make a quick stop by the restrooms if needed and get some popcorn and soda."

Even though we had just eaten, the smell of buttered popcorn wafting through my nostrils while walking to the theater door had sent a signal to my brain that there was still room for popcorn. It was an absolute must in my family. We only had popcorn on certain occasions, and watching a terrific movie was one of them.

Alan asked Dad, "Can Taylor and I go for popcorn?"

"Sure," answered Dad. "Mom and I will stay here. You guys know the rule, stick together. You go straight to the concession stand and straight back, no detours allowed. Got it?"

"Got it," said Alan.

"Got it," I replied.

We made our way to the concession stand. There were so many choices. Row after row of delectable, scrumptious, tasty candy stared back at me through the clear glass display. I wanted them all, but popcorn would be fine.

My parents had been pretty generous taking us to the movies. Our family had a monthly budget and I knew this was probably taking a big chunk of that money. Dad and Mom were saving up money for the future. That part was a little confusing to me but I knew it was important to save.

"What do you want Taylor?" asked Alan.

"Just popcorn will do," I answered.

"You don't want a drink to go with your popcorn?" asked Alan with a puzzled look.

"Are you getting one? How much money does it cost?" I asked Alan as I started scanning the menu on the wall.

"It's okay. Dad said if we didn't get any candy to go with the popcorn we each can have a drink instead," said Alan.

"So I would like a small soda to go with my popcorn please," I stated.

We moved up the line fairly quick. There was one boy in front of us. As the lady behind the counter handed him his root beer soda, it slipped between his fingers and the entire soda spilled on the front of his shirt and pants. Jumping back, the boy stepped hard on my big toe.

Things like that always seem to happen to me. I did a little dance trying to make my poor toe stop hurting. The boy looked at me, shrugged his shoulders, and said "sorry" just before he ran to the bathroom. We were helped by another woman behind the counter while they tried to clean up the mess as fast as possible. Once we were loaded down with popcorn and sodas, we headed for our movie.

I was trying my best not to spill anything; looking down so I wouldn't step on the back of Alan's heel, I followed him blindly into the theater door. Our movie was in number eight.

It was dark inside. My eyes had already adjusted to the light out by the concession stand so I couldn't see very well for several seconds. I tried looking up to where I thought we had sat down but I couldn't see anybody.

"Alan, where are Mom and Dad?" I asked.

"I don't know," replied Alan.

He was looking all around the room but there didn't appear to be anyone in here. We both looked at the screen at the same time. Clearly there was something being played on the screen but it looked like just some really old footage because all I saw were these squiggly white lines on the screen, nothing else. I turned around and looked up at the room where the movie was being projected from. I thought I saw someone looking down at us but when I rubbed my eyes and looked again, no one was there.

"Did you come to the right theater Alan? We *are* in theater number eight, aren't we?" I questioned Alan.

Alan sighed. "Oh, that's the problem. This is number nine, for a minute there I thought something weird was going on again."

I knew what he was talking about. Last summer we had taken a vacation to Ocean City, Maryland where we had met Nadia and Trundell. That had been a wild adventure to the Land of Spark.

No adventures for me today. I just wanted to see my movie. "Let's go," I urged Alan. I started to move toward the walkway back out to the theater door when something caught both our eyes. A small projection of a path suddenly appeared on the screen.

"Look," said Alan.

"I see it," I replied. "But what does it mean?"

It looked so out of place. I mean there wasn't any sound, no trailer, no "Please dispose of your trash in the proper receptacles," no trivia questions to entertain you while you waited—just a stone pathway that wound its ways through the forest.

Alan and I were drawn to the screen. That's the only reason I can come up with to explain what happened next. We walked over to the lowest portion of the screen to take a closer look. I looked back and up into the projector room to see if the person was there but I couldn't see anyone. I walked up a few rows and I lowered the seat of the closest chair and stood up on it. The seat cushion was way too cushiony so my feet sort of sank down in the cushion. I scrambled up on the armrest; that was much better.

I gained some height, looked up again, and saw a shadow but couldn't make out much more.

"What are you doing Taylor? Get down!" Alan wailed.

"I thought I saw someone," I said while trying to balance myself on the armrest.

I could see the light stream from the projector room just above me. Something intrigued me about the light. I slowly raised my arm toward it. As soon as I put my hand near the light, I could feel a strange sensation. My fingers were the first thing to enter the light. They tingled. My whole hand and part of my arm were now surrounded by the light. To my amazement, my feet left the arm chair and I was moving toward the screen. Right then my only thought was 'how cool is this,' I felt as light as a Blue Jay. I could hear Alan screaming something but I seemed helpless to stop my forward momentum.

Alan stood on one of the chairs and tried to grab my legs. He just missed. I was almost to the screen now. Alan ran in front of me and stood on the armrest of the chair directly in front of the screen. He took a flying leap into the air as high as he could and grabbed both my feet.

Chapter Three

In the next breath I knew we were somewhere else. It was a dizzying ride, one minute I was holding popcorn and soda at the theater and the next I found myself standing on a path with Alan that I did not recognize.

"Oh no, here we go again," I shouted to the universe. "Not today, today I want to see my terrific movie, eat my delicious popcorn, and drink my ice-cold soda!"

"Me too," said Alan looking around. "But I don't think we have a choice."

Wherever here was, it was noisy. I could hear what sounded like birds chirping all around us.

"What have we gotten ourselves into this time?" questioned Alan.

That's when we heard it. I knew this could not be good. There was a low grinding sound coming from somewhere straight ahead of us. A loud, distinct whistle, two toots in a row. Alan grabbed my hand and took off to investigate. I tried yanking my hand out of his but I knew it was useless, Alan loved adventures, what can I say.

The path we found ourselves on was a light colored stone path, dirt mostly with light smooth stones mixed in. On either side laid freshly cut grass with flower beds here and there filled with tall flowers that resembled Black-eyed Susans. Nice.

I let Alan lead me in the direction where the noise came from. As we turned the corner, we both saw a huge train. It looked like a steam engine, the kind that people used to ride on a long time ago. Like the type Alan and I had seen at the museum.

We could hear the conductor shouting over the crowd of people, "If you want to board for Baltimore, you must do so now. We leave promptly in 4 minutes

at twelve o'clock. The next train to Baltimore will be tomorrow morning at eight o'clock sharp."

There were a few people still left on the ramp. I noticed their dress was strange. A woman holding a baby in her arms had a full length dress on that flared out at the bottom. The man standing beside her had a bowler hat on. Either these people were dressed for a masquerade ball or we were definitely someplace else.

"A-l-l aboard," shouted the conductor.

"Let's go," said Alan.

"Are you insane?" I asked Alan. "We can't get on!"

"Why not?" Alan asked.

"Well, for one thing we don't have any money?" I retorted.

"I have some," replied Alan. "I have change from the concession stand."

I yanked on his sleeve. "I want to go back and see the movie with Mom and Dad," I said desperately.

"You know we are supposed to go. You know that. C'mon Taylor, let's get on." Alan walked to the line where a half a dozen passengers were boarding.

I just rolled my eyes. I walked over to where Alan was now standing, waiting to board this steam-powered train going to Baltimore. I carefully looked around trying to figure out where we were and who needed our help.

There were steep steps up to board the train. We sat down in two aisle seats. They were hard wooden benches really, not very comfortable. In fact, the train's interior looked old and worn.

Alan and I, along with our mom, dad, and uncle Bart had taken the train once all the way to Florida. The train had really nice seats and a dining car. I remember how nicely decorated it had been. This train looked colorless and uncomfortable.

A lady across from me was staring at me. I looked away twice, like I was interested in the view out the window, but each time I looked back, her eyes were staring straight into mine.

"What?" I mumbled.

"What?" Alan inquired, turning his head to look at me.

I whispered into his ear, "That lady over there is staring at me."

Alan slowly raised his head and looked across the aisle. Before he could say anything further the lady started to speak.

"What sort of attire might that be that you have on?" she asked.

I looked down at myself. I had a dark blue tee-shirt and a pair of jeans on. I wore a pair of open-toed brown sandals. I didn't see anything out of place. No tissue stuck to the bottom of my shoe and my zipper was zipped all the way up. I checked.

She was pointing to my jeans.

"Are those bloomers?" she questioned.

"Bloomers?" I asked. I looked to Alan for help.

"Um, yes ma'am they're bloomers," answered Alan.

"I'm so excited! I've never seen any bloomers that look like that." The look on the ladies' face was one of pure joy.

I didn't get it; they were just an old pair of jeans that had seen better days. There was even a teeny tiny hole at the knee.

"Where is your destination, if I may inquire?" asked the pretty lady.

She had a round face with big blue eyes. Her complexion was very light, like she never sat in the sun for very long. Her dress was floor length and a dark shade of grey. The material looked itchy.

"Um, Baltimore," I made up.

"I am going there as well," she excitedly answered. "My name is Annabelle," she stated while extending her gloved hand.

We both shook her hand. Then we shook the hand of her companion. The woman sitting next to her had not spoken. She appeared to be much shorter and stocky. She had long hair I think. It was hard to make out such features because she had her hair tied up in a bun and she wore a scowl on her face. She was huddled inside a grey wool blanket. I was so hot I couldn't imagine how hot it would be inside the itchy looking blanket.

"Charlotte and I are headed for the rally on Pratt Street," stated Annabelle. "Are you two going there as well?"

"Yes, as a matter of fact we are," answered Alan.

I didn't even have a chance to open my mouth. I nudged his foot with mine. What was wrong with Alan? We didn't even know what the rally was about.

Annabelle touched Charlotte's arm and sat up straighter, "We are with the NAWS. We hope to meet Mrs. Hooker."

I had no clue what NAWS was but I wasn't going to ask. Annabelle must have seen the confused look on my face.

"You don't know what NAWS is? She looked questioningly at Charlotte. It is the National American Woman Suffrage Association," stated Annabelle. "Where did you say you were from?" queried Annabelle.

"Annapolis," answered Alan quickly. He tried to change the subject so Annabelle wouldn't ask too many questions about us. He didn't need to because the conductor approached and asked everyone for their tickets. I let Alan handle it because he had the money and I wanted to see what was out the window that had caught my eye.

Several teams of mules were pulling a wagon out of a large muddy rut. I guess they were being used like a tow truck would be used to pull a car out.

Just then we heard a loud whistle. We were coming into the station. The train was slowing down. I could hear the brakes screeching and a loud hissing sound that startled me. I think that was the steam being released.

Annabelle and Charlotte began gathering their personal belongings.

"Well it was very nice talking with you," nodded Annabelle.

Charlotte nodded as well. She then used her hands to speak to Annabelle. She was using sign language. Now I understood why she never spoke. I thought maybe she was shy or just plain rude. I guess I shouldn't be so quick to judge people. Mom always says, "You shouldn't dislike someone until you have a very good reason, and when you have one you should rethink it."

They waved as they departed the train.

"Come on Taylor, let's get off too," Alan insisted as he pulled on my arm.

I let Alan lead me off the train. I was getting hungry and I smelled something good as we stepped away from the platform. As I was trying to identify the direction of the great smell of food, I noticed there were a small group of boys standing in the shade not far from us. They looked up as we approached.

"You sure are dressed funny. You a girl ain't ya?" asked the boy sitting on a low branch of the shade tree. The boy was pointing at me. He spat this gooey, thick, disgusting brown substance down on the ground beside me. His words made me feel uncomfortable. What did he mean? Did I look that strange?

Alan stepped in front of me. "She's wearing bloomers—that's all."

The boy said, "Sorry. I ain't ever seen no bloomers before. I heard bout 'em from my ma but I never seen any. My name's John and this here is Jake and Billy," John pointed to the other boys with him. Both boys were shoeless. I looked down at the ground. Rocks, small pebbles, and a lot of uneven ground everywhere I looked. I was feeling grateful I had a pair of shoes on.

John looked to be about 11 or 12 I'd guess with a mop full of thick blond hair and the bluest eyes that were slightly large. Jake was a definite redhead with freckles and Billy looked much darker with dark hair, dark eyes, and dark skin.

I whispered to Alan, "What's he chewing on?"

"I think its chewing tobacco."

"Yuck and double yuck. That's disgusting. Doesn't he know how bad that is for your health?"

"I don't think they knew about the dangers of chewing tobacco back then," answered Alan just above a whisper.

"Hey, what you guys conferring about?" asked the boy named Jake as he too spit some of the yucky substance on the ground.

"Actually I was asking about that brown stuff in your mouth," I bravely spoke up.

"What—this?" John asked as he spit some more out. "My pa let me have some. I already done all my chores," he proudly exclaimed. "I'm gonna be a baseball player. Mrs. Talbot says she ain't ever seen anybody throw a ball as fast as I can. Mrs. Talbot knows about things like that because her boy, Linwood, is a player for the Double Diamonds. Next time he comes home for a spell, Mrs. Talbot is gonna introduce us."

The other boys shook their heads in agreement.

I just couldn't help myself, I felt compelled to speak out. "You know, that stuff can make horrible sores in your mouth and it can really hurt you. It's very bad for your body."

All the boys turned their attention to me. No one said a word.

"Um… well could you point us in the right direction to find a place to eat?" Alan interjected.

The boys all laughed.

John said, "How'd you know my pa had sores in his mouth? You're not from around here are ya?"

"Actually, no," I replied.

John said, "You could try Mary's Kitchen Corner over there." He pointed with his finger to a location down the road a bit.

The road was dusty and dry and it was of my opinion that it probably was a mess when it rained. There were pot holes, a lot of pot holes everywhere.

"I warn you, Miss Mary is very strict about how you eat," said Jake.

"Yeah, you have to sit up straight and lay the red checkered napkin across your lap with the top tucked in under your chin," piped in John. "It'll cost you 20 cents for dinner, 22 cents for supper. You're in luck 'cause Miss Mary has a special today. Dinner is half price but you have to hurry 'cause it looks like dinnertime is almost over."

"Thanks," I replied. I wasn't sure what he meant by "dinner" and "supper." Weren't they the same thing? Alan and I *were* sort of hungry. I wondered if they would take the coins Alan had in his pocket.

Chapter Four

After thanking the boys we walked down the street to Mary's Kitchen Corner and sat down at one of the outdoor tables. I immediately saw a beautiful woman looking over at us.

There was just something about her. I couldn't quite put my finger on it; her hair was a dark shade of brown, her eyes a light shade of blue. She wore a hat that had a broad rim with feathers and a very nice smile that lit up her face.

She knew our names, called to us from across the way. Alan and I just stared at each other.

"Well Taylor," she said as she nodded once in my direction. "Well Alan," she said as she nodded toward Alan. "May I join you?"

"Sure, sure," we both answered at the same time.

She walked over to the table and sat down. "I am Bella. I watch over the Land of Baltimore. I need you Taylor, and you Alan, to help me."

"What can we do?" I asked. This was pretty unbelievable—all of it. I would have thought it was a dream except that we had already visited the Land of Spark and I knew it wasn't a dream.

"You are needed to help the good people here." Her smile broadened. "You have a certain talent for helping I am told."

"We do?" I questioned.

"Will you help us?" Bella asked.

"Sure," I said.

"Of course," chimed in Alan.

Bella took a deep breath. "Well I am certain that the wizard, Jalabar, has his spies all around. He is a very bad wizard and he will receive his punishment once the wizard's council reconvenes. Everything is in a huge upheaval at this point in time. Unfortunately, by the time I can bring him before the council he will have already taken control of the Land of Baltimore. I cannot allow Jalabar to gain control over the Land of Baltimore and I need your help to make sure he doesn't accomplish that."

A lot of questions were running through my mind. How did she know us? How could we help? How did we keep ending up in strange lands?

Alan spoke up. "Excuse me but I am a little confused. How can we help you exactly?"

Bella just smiled. "You and your sister, Alan, can help by securing the key. The key, you see, is what Jalabar needs to open the Chest of Treasures. He seeks more power. Power that once in the hands of Jalabar will forever change the Land of Baltimore I'm afraid. Only children, such as yourselves, can retrieve the key, and return it to the keepers of the key. They are the protectors."

Miss Mary came over to our table and wanted to take our order. As Alan and I were trying to figure out if we had enough money to buy a complete meal, Bella told us we needed our bellies full to accomplish our mission. She insisted she would take care of the bill.

Alan and I got the roast beef special that came with home fries, gravy and a biscuit on the side. We each got a tall glass of milk that tasted way creamier than the milk we have at home. I wondered if Mom could get some of this creamy milk at the grocery store. I doubted that though.

I elbowed Alan. "What?" Alan inquired.

"Look how the other patrons are eating," I muttered.

The patrons were using their biscuits to get all the gravy, rather than a spoon.

"Hey, that looks like a good idea," said Alan. He immediately put his spoon down and used the biscuit to "slop" up the gravy.

"Try it Taylor," Alan insisted.

"Okay," answered Taylor.

I took the edge of the biscuit and used it as a sort of spoon and scooped up the gravy onto the biscuit.

"Hey this works pretty well," Taylor stated.

By the time they were finished there was no gravy left on the plate. Mom would have been proud. Bella ordered pie; we each had a slice of Shoofly pie. Yummy!

We said our goodbyes and began following the directions Bella gave us. She said to find the one who had swing.

“Alan I have no idea what Bella’s clue means, do you?” I asked.

“No, but that doesn’t mean we won’t figure it out Taylor.”

After walking around for a long time without any progress that I could tell, the three boys, John, Jake, and Billy joined us down by the river. I sat on some crates and leaned my head back to take a quick break while the boys discussed fishing. *My feet hurt, how in the world can the boys walk around all day without shoes?* I wondered.

After resting a bit, we headed back into town. The place was really beautiful. The trees were full and lush. There didn’t seem to be any dead or dying plants anywhere. Every plant had new growth on it and the blooms were twice the size I remembered seeing back home. The grass was thick, no bare spots that I could see. Even the water down by the riverbank was clear. Something I rarely saw where we lived.

I remembered my mother telling Alan and I, that the water nearest us, the bay water and ocean water, used to be clear, back when she was a little girl. I never saw that; now days it was not an unusual sight that the water was cloudy, or murky, along with the occasional piece of trash.

Alan and I belonged to the recycling club at our school. We had cleanup days down at the beach, visits to local nature centers to learn how recycling helps save wildlife and the environment, and we had a booth stand at many local events where we talked about time and money saving tips to recycle.

I almost tripped while walking and thinking. As the boys and I were crossing the street, or rather a dirt road, I saw there was a man talking, or rather talking really loudly, with another man standing on the boardwalk not far behind us. They didn't appear to be paying attention to their surroundings and thus did not hear the shouting from behind.

We all turned quickly to see two horses that were dragging the rigging for a wagon down the street. The horses had a crazed, wild look in their eyes. Galloping at top speed, they were coming straight for the man still standing in the street. The two men seemed to be arguing and were oblivious to the commotion.

"Alan, look. The man," I screamed.

Alan bellowed to John, "Help him John."

John was the closest one to the man. He quickly ran to him and knocked him over and into the horse trough and then jumped up on the boardwalk. The horses pulled up just short of ramming the trough and headed farther down the road before several men were able to bring the team of horses to a stop.

The man came up spitting water out of his mouth.

"By the saints, what in world did you do that for?" said the man. He looked somewhat like a drown rat with his hair sleeked back against his forehead; his clothes were drenched and dripping, all while he was trying to bring his leg over the rim. While trying to stand he slipped and fell back into the water. He gave up and just sat there staring up at John.

The other man, the one who had been safely on the boardwalk behind the horse trough announced, "That boy just saved your hide, Wee Willie."

Wee Willie looked around as if he had just woke up. He looked down the street and saw the team of horses being attended to. Then he looked over at us kids.

"What is your name son?" asked Wee Willie.

"My name is John, sir."

"Well, John, my name is Wee Willie. I'm a baseball player here in town. I know a lot of people will want to thank you for saving this old fool's hide today. I am expected to play in today's game for the pennant.

All the kids spoke up at once and no one could understand a word said.

Wee Willie spoke up. "Hush ya'll. I need some help getting out of this horse trough.

"Yes, sir. Right away, sir," said John.

We all moved closer toward Wee Willie, just in case he slipped again. The water looked a little nasty to me. *I hope he takes a bath before he plays.*

Alan whispered to me, "That's Wee Willie."

"Wow. So were we supposed to help him?" I asked.

Alan whispered back, "I guess so. This is so cool."

"Well, John, how would you and your friends like to join me for a sweet treat and then head over to the field to watch the game?" asked Wee Willie.

John turned to Billy and said, "Ain't this great?"

Billy whispered into his ear, "Don't be a knuckle-head. We ain't got no money."

John turned to Wee Willie. "Gee, I would love to Mr. Wee Willie, but my friends and I don't have any money," answered John.

"No need for money John, it's my treat. I owe you my life after all," replied Wee Willie with a wink.

A huge smile crossed John's face. He looked over at Alan and I. "You two seem to be my lucky charm."

Chapter Five

After eating some yummy candy corn, we arrived at the game a short time later. Alan and I sat down farthest from the aisle, while John, Jake, and Billy sat nearest the aisle. Usually, Alan and I would sit on the aisle seats because it was easier to get up and go, if you know what I mean.

I was looking around when I heard… "Get your popcorn..." Kid Alert. I love popcorn. It is by far my biggest personal weakness. Especially if it has melted butter drizzled on top. Yum. Oh, and chocolate too. No self-respecting kid went without chocolate for very long.

Next to me sat two women who looked very excited to be at the game. I said hello to them because they seemed very friendly. They told me they were from out of town visiting some friends and family here in Baltimore. Their names were Sarah and Daisy. We exchanged small talk or what my mom called "pleasantries," and then became engrossed in the game.

They were playing against the Spiders. Wee Willie was up. Upon delivery of the pitch, Wee Willie hit the ball, or rather didn't. I mean he knocked it sort of but the ball did a funny bounce and he ran to first base. He was safe. The crowd cheered.

Alan leaned over, closer to me and said, "That's called the "Baltimore Chop" Wee Willie is famous for it. I can't believe I got to see him do the "Baltimore Chop." This is so cool Taylor." Alan elbowed me. I could see the excitement in his expression as his eyes lit up.

I thought it was a nail-biter but Alan thought it was a slam dunk. Baltimore won the pennant and the crowd was going wild. Everyone jumped up and down. A few people not far from our seats were screaming, "Wee Willie, Wee Willie," so I started to chant too. So did Alan and the boys. We were all smiles.

Sometime later as the crowd started to disperse Alan and I started to talk among ourselves about how we would go about trying to find Swing.

"How are we going to find Swing? I don't have any idea where to start looking," I said to Alan.

"I know. Swing could be just about anything from a pet frog to a wooden swing. Maybe we should ask the boys when we get out of here."

"Okay," I said thinking about what or who Swing might be.

"Pardon me, Miss Taylor," stated Sarah. "Miss Daisy says you need to go to the livery stable to find Swing."

I looked over at Daisy. "Thanks," I replied.

"You're welcome my dear," exclaimed Daisy.

I opened my mouth to speak, to ask her what or who Swing was when she rose from her seat and stood up.

"Good luck," Miss Daisy said.

"Sarah, we really mustn't be late getting back to the house, you know how your mama feels about being tardy. I wouldn't want to make a bad impression."

Sarah said, "Oh don't worry Daisy, she knows we are at the game."

"Nonetheless, let's be about our business," stated Daisy. "Excuse us."

"Thank you again. Nice meeting you," I said to Sarah and Daisy.

"Goodbye," exclaimed Sarah politely.

Daisy smiled and said, "Goodbye."

We all stood up so the women could get around us to the aisle where they hurried on their way.

"Hey Alan, Daisy told me we could find Swing at the livery stable, whatever that means."

"Is Swing a who or a what? Did you ask her?" questioned Alan.

"No I didn't have a chance, they were in a hurry. At least we now know where to start looking," I said.

"Good work," said Alan.

"Thanks."

After the game we went a short distance with the boys. They needed to get home. One of the boys was an orphan that had recently been adopted by a nice couple here in town. Originally, the couple had lived in Iowa where the Orphan Train had stopped. Mr. Wilson, Billy's adopted father, had met the train looking for a boy of strong health and good stature to help around with the chores as he and Mrs. Wilson were getting up in age. With no children of their own they decided to adopt one of the children.

Billy explained the Children's Aid Society had arranged for him to ride the Orphan Train to Iowa from New York City. His new parents had just moved to the Land of Baltimore.

"Yeah, I loved New York City," boasted Billy. His expression changed, and a look of sadness replaced his happy face, "But...I was always hungry—so hungry."

The look on Billy's face had said it all.

"It must have been horrible to be hungry," I said.

"The cold was worse. Sometimes, at night, the cold would consume me. No matter what, I just couldn't get warm. I saw the entire rich folk walk by me and pretend they didn't see me. I tried asking for money so I could buy my own food but that didn't work very well. I was dirty looking and just so hungry. So I stole an apple off the end of the cart of Mr. Osborne's stand. I didn't get caught. Later, as I was eating it, I felt so guilty."

Billy choked up a little but seemed to gather his wits. He continued. "I grabbed another apple two days later but I knew I would come to a bad end if I kept taking things that didn't belong to me so I agreed to get on the train. I'm really happy I did too. My new ma and pa are really nice to me and feed me real good. I have made a vow never to steal again, no matter what."

"One day I up and started balling at the dinner table like a baby. I confessed to my new ma and pa I was a bad kid because I had stolen some food once or twice. We talked and talked about it and they told me I wasn't a bad kid. I worked extra chores for a whole year and all the earned money was sent to

Mr. Osborne with a letter of apology. He wrote me back just last week accepting my apology."

My sympathy instincts flared. I had never experienced hunger. I couldn't imagine how it must feel. No one talked as we walked down the street. I couldn't think of anything to say. I guess no one else could either.

We said goodbye to our three new friends, promising to meet up with them tomorrow, and went our separate way. I was exhausted and wanted to rest a bit before we saved the Land of Baltimore.

There was a sign above the only boarding house in town. It was called, Molly's Boarding House. Bella had paid for the room. Both Alan and I had told her we would pay for our own room if we needed to spend the night but she had yet again insisted. She said it was the least she could do to repay us for helping.

Miss Molly seemed very satisfied when we told her our names. She said she was pleased that we were staying at her boarding house and told us to just let her know if we needed anything at all.

Rising the next morning feeling rested and hungry, we were happy to smell home cooked food as we walked down the stairs. A hardy meal of eggs, bacon, and biscuits filled our bellies for the work ahead.

We decided to walk around the town. It turned out to be a meet and greet because everywhere we went the townsfolk seemed interested in us. The people of the Land of Baltimore were very friendly and helpful.

As we continued on our walk we saw several buildings with windows open. I twitched my nose. It smelled here, a most unpleasant smell I might add. Fishy actually—fishy, yuck.

"You smell that?" Alan asked.

"Yeah. I think I might gag. What are they doing in there?"

"I think this is Cannery Row," answered Alan.

"What's a Cannery Row?" I asked.

"I think this is the place where people can goods. You know, like oysters," replied Alan.

"Yuck." I didn't like oysters to eat but I knew many people loved the taste. I liked to help our local program that encouraged homeowners to raise oyster larvae. It was part of a plan to help restore the Chesapeake Bay. Oysters helped to clean the bay, and there were too few of them left to clean the water.

This part of Baltimore looked vastly different. It was a little dirty, smelly, and too crowded. Alan explained they made children work alongside the adults for very long hours of the day before laws were put into place to protect children.

"That's terrible," I said.

"I know," Alan agreed. "That's why Mom and Dad are always telling us to be thankful for all we have, and to not complain about the things we don't."

I guess, if I am being totally honest with myself, I really sort-of let those particular phrases go in one ear and out the other, most of the time. Mostly because I have heard it too many times now. I guess I really did have a lot of things to be thankful for.

We continued walking until we saw what looked like a huge barn. It was near the edge of town that had a sign above it that said, C.W. and Sons, Livery Stable.

When we got closer and peered inside I saw stalls lined with straw, some had horses in them and there were all kinds of tack lying around. There was a man busy shoeing a horse.

"Wow, look Taylor, I've never seen a horse having a shoe put on before," exclaimed Alan.

Alan looked excited. I studied the horse carefully. He didn't *look* like he was in any pain but how could that be? There were nail thingies that the blacksmith was driving into the horse's hoof. The man paid us no attention; rather, he was talking to the horse.

"Matilda, you know you are a good 'ole horse, faithful too. You and me, we had lots of good times. Yes sireee, we had some good times together. You know I reckon we have ridden over to Catonsville to visit Miss Coleen maybe over a dozen times by now. Guess that's why you need new shoes. There, you're as good as new."

The man stood up letting the horse put her leg back down. He backed away and gave the horse a good inspection. Seemingly satisfied, he patted the horse's rump, led the horse over to a stall and took off her head piece and reins. He took an apple out of his pocket and let the horse take it out of his open hand. The horse raised her head to get a look at us.

The man turned his head. "Howdy folks. How may I help you young folks today?" the man inquired.

"Hello," we both answered.

Alan spoke up. "Um, we just wanted to watch you. I hope we didn't disturb you," said Alan.

The man laughed. "No, you didn't disturb me. Just shoeing Matilda, that's all. He extended his hand. "My name's Carson but everyone just calls me Smithy."

Alan shook his hand. "My name is Alan, and this is my sister, Taylor."

I shook his hand as well.

Another man walked into the livery stable yelling, "Smithy how ya doing?"

This man was tall—really tall. His size dwarfed everyone around him. He was skinny as a rail with long red hair. At least I thought it was long. It sat just below his shoulders.

"Sorry didn't see you had customers," he said as he approached them.

"Na, these kids just wanted to watch me," Smithy said with a smile.

"Who wants to watch *you*?" teased the man.

"Sorry, where are my manners? My name is James but everyone just calls me Swing."

Hooray, I think we just found our clue.

Alan smiled, "I'm Alan, and this is my sister, Taylor." We shook hands with Swing.

"Well kids it was nice meeting you but I have to get back to work," Smithy said. "Maybe you can ask Swing what it is he does."

"Sure. You kids come with me."

Swing walked out of the livery stable and over to a wooden bench. He sat down and reached for what looked like an old rag and wiped his forehead with it.

"Sure is a hot one today," he said looking up at the sun.

Taylor saw a huge pile of cut firewood. Swing stood up and put a big piece of wood on a nearby stump. He picked up his axe and swung it in the air and brought the axe down so fast, so hard, the piece of wood split right in the middle. He picked up the two pieces and set them aside. He split several more pieces before he sat down again.

"Wow. That looks really hard, but you make it seem like it's easy," I declared.

"Oh, I have been doing it for a long time. I get tired sometimes, which is why I sit a spell in between," he replied.

"Hey, that's why they call you Swing," I laughed.

"Yep," is all he said.

He resumed working. Quietly, Alan and I started talking about our mission.

"Well, he is definitely Swing, Taylor. Maybe we should just ask him what happened to the key."

We waited until Swing took another short break to talk with him.

"Excuse me, Swing, but my brother and I would like to talk with you about something important. We are looking for the key."

Swing's look totally changed. He went from a nice man wiping his forehead with a rag, to a man ready to do battle. He sat up straight and moved his axe closer to him.

"Who are you, and don't even try to tell me no lie," Swing demanded.

"No, sir. We want to help you. We were sent by Bella," stated Alan.

"How do you know Bella?" he asked.

Bella had told us what we needed to say to help convince him we were friendly.

Alan looked around to see if anyone was close by. "Zanzar," Alan said just above a whisper. Zanzar was the code word that Bella had told us to use to prove that we were helping her.

"Oh." He seemed relieved.

"Smithy," he hollered. "Come out here."

Smithy came right away. "Is something wrong?" he asked. His brown hair was plastered against his head with sweat visible from his forehead to his sweat-soaked shirt. He looked at us anxiously as he wiped the sweat running down his face with an old rag.

"No. These youngins just asked me about the key," stated Swing. And, he added lowering his voice, "They said, 'Zanzar.' Bella sent them."

Smithy sat down in the dirt. He lowered his voice.

"We need help finding the key alright. I am Swing's brother-in-law, and our family helps his family keep the key safe," Smithy explained.

"You see my Mrs., Mary that is, had taken the key off because it started to turn red. It was getting too hot to wear around her neck. Mary has been secretly wearing it on a long chain around her neck hidden from prying eyes for years. This is the very first time the key has turned hot to the touch," stated Swing.

Swing continued, "Mary works Mondays and Wednesdays at Mr. Cameron's General Store. She was forced to take it off for a spell so she laid it behind the counter, tucked away under some sewing material, and stayed in the room with it. A couple hours later when she went back to check and see if it had cooled down enough to put back on, it was gone. A window close by was open."

"The key must be found. The key opens the Chest of Treasures. It must not fall into the hands of the wizard, Jalabar," insisted Smithy.

"We will do everything possible to recover the key," I reassured Smithy and Swing.

"What is in the Chest of Treasures?" asked Alan.

"I don't know," answered Swing. "All we know is that if the contents were to fall into the wrong hands we would all be doomed."

"How long have you watched over the key?" I inquired.

"For many generations my family has watched over it," stated Swing. "And," he added, "never before has the key changed its properties in any way."

"We will do everything we can to get it back," I emphasized.

"What does Zanzar mean?" Alan asked.

"Actually, Zanzar, a very powerful wizard from centuries ago, was a good and wise wizard," stated Swing.

Alan added, "Well, we will get right on it. Do you have anything else you can tell us that might help us find it?"

"Well, I can tell you this: my grandfather, one of the keepers of the key, told me that his father told him that the key is magical, and so, 'it will sing for one who is searching when near,'" Swing explained.

"Sing?!" Alan and I said at the same time.

"Do you know where the Chest of Treasures lies?" asked Swing.

"Us? I thought you knew?" quizzed Alan.

"No. I only know that the Chest of Treasures is hidden 'by the light of the moon one can see through the shadows; no more, no less, than one pony high.'"

Alan and I exchanged puzzled looks.

"Thank you for trusting us," I told Swing.

Swing and Smithy just nodded their heads in unison.

Chapter Six

We left Swing and Smithy and headed down the street. Alan and I walked over to Mr. Cameron's General Store. Once, a couple of summers ago, our family had traveled out west. Our great aunt, Zinna, was getting married. We decided as a family it would be fun to travel by car and to leave a week and a half earlier than the wedding. We would stop along the way and see many sites that would be fun to explore. Mom and Dad were history buffs and loved to stop at little out-of-the-way places that told a story about our past. Our parents had planned, months in advance, all the possible places to stop.

One of the places, we all had voted to stop at was an old western ghost town. It was unreal. I mean the way they lived back then: riding stage coaches, no electricity, no running water, and no video games. I shuddered at the thought. How did they survive?

And the worst part in my mind, a one-room school house. It would have been horrible to be the youngest kid in the school room. All the big kids would know all the answers. They probably walked around barefoot too.

The dusty road had tumbleweeds rolling along in the breeze. Signs above the doors were hand painted, not like the business signs where we lived. We walked into several of the buildings to see how people lived a long time ago. One building was a saloon. You could walk about six feet inside. A wide banister prevented you from going all the way inside, probably to prevent tourists from knocking things over. There was a piano just inside the door with a mannequin on a stool with his hands on the keyboard. He looked like he was singing while playing a tune.

The saloon also served as the dentist's office, with another mannequin working on a man seated in the chair. The man seated had a large cloth napkin tucked under his chin with his mouth wide open and his hands gripping the sides of the chair.

I asked Mom, "Do you think the dentist was gentle like Dr. Pendergrass is?" Dr. Pendergrass, our dentist, is really nice and gentle. I loved going to the dentist because Dr. Pendergrass had two treat drawers. One for the young kids and one for the older kids; I got to pick one treat from the older kids drawer now. Last time we went there for a cleaning I picked a mini dry-erase board. I still have it sitting on my dresser.

My mom had answered, "No honey I don't think so, I think Dr. Pendergrass is much gentler."

It looked like the dentist had a pair of tweezers, but much larger, and he was about to extract one of the patient's teeth. Yikes.

Another building looked to be a home. Inside the door I looked around carefully. I saw a wash basin sitting near the door. I knew it was a wash basin because my dad had told us about his great-grandfather, William.

He said back in those days most families didn't have running water so they kept a wash basin near the door. You could wash your hands in the basin, dry your hands with the small towel close by and then open the door, throw the dirty water off the porch down into the grass and then go get some more, clean water, for the next person from the pump around back. The 'pump' was really a hand pump you had to push and pull until some water came out through the spigot and into the bucket. The pump got the water from the deep underground well.

It sounded like a lot of work just to wash your hands. There were a raggedy set of curtains hanging on the window. The small wooden table had three chairs that looked old and drab. A small plate sat in front of a man who had a pipe hanging from his mouth. Yuck. A fireplace was the centerpiece in the room with a long large wooden mantle above it. A rifle lay across the table nearby. At the far end of the small room sat a violin. I imagined music was one of the only forms of entertainment back then; probably square dancing too. The floor was wooden and the walls were old and dirty.

Near the end of the tour we came upon the general store with its huge hand-painted sign above the entry. Several old-timey photos hung on the walls of real people standing in the very same general store more than a hundred fifty years earlier.

The people were dressed very differently. Looking down, I had on a pair of khaki shorts, a tee-shirt, and sandals on. The women in the photos had dresses that touched the ground, and some of them had hats on as well. They had long sleeves and ruffles on the collar of their dresses with a brooch pinned on top. That sure did appear to be really hot attire. I was suddenly really glad I didn't live back then.

The men seemed to be dressed somewhat similar to what most men wore today I thought. The clothes did look itchy though, but basically they had long pants on with cloth shirts on. Some of the men in the photos had suspenders on, some wore hats.

As I walked further into the store, I noticed the store didn't have banisters to block you from entering; this store was a real working general store. The people working behind the counters had period dress on and the cash registers were the old-timey cash registers from long ago. The counters were much higher than any counters I had seen. They were huge wooden cases that opened from the back. Several workers were helping customers. The customers pointed to what they wanted through the glass panes. Piles of candy and trinkets were inside those cases.

Most stores that I have been to like the big box store, Pam's, you just walked down the long aisles and picked what you wanted from an industrial type warehouse. This general store had a different kind of feel to it. It was much smaller and the merchandise very different. I liked it. The atmosphere in here was cozy. Over by the far side of the store, near the pot belly stove, sat two chairs with a checkerboard on top of the table in between. Alan and I played three games before we got up and picked one item each to take back home.

Mr. Cameron's General Store, however, looked very much the same as the general store in the Old West Ghost Town. It was really a nice store. I zeroed in on the peppermint sticks and a few lollipops right away.

A very pretty lady stood behind the counter. She smiled at us and said, "I take it you are the new strangers in town."

"Yes. I guess you could say that," Alan answered. "My name is Alan and this here," as he pointed in my direction, "is my sister, Taylor."

"Pleased to meet you—Alan and Taylor."

"Thank you," I stated.

"Thank you," said Alan.

"My name is Mary. How can I help you children today?" She was looking at another customer in the store looking at some bolts of fabric displayed on a nearby table.

"Just looking around for right now," I said.

Mary walked over to help the customer at the fabric table. The customer bought a yard of floral print fabric and left.

"I thought she'd never leave," Mary expressed. "Swing stopped by a few minutes ago and told me about you two. How can I help you with your investigation?"

"Well can you please tell us what happened exactly?"

"Sure. I came in to work on Monday, just like I usually do; I had just sat out some new pretty fabrics, when I felt the key hanging on my chain get warm, really warm. I was forced to take it off. I put it behind the counter hidden under some rags. I was sure no one saw me. I didn't know what else to do. I feel so bad that it has gone missing; Swing and his family trusted me to protect it."

"It's not your fault. You had to take it off," I reminded her.

"Thanks, but until the key is found I'm afraid I will remain upset," Mary said. "So, to continue…I was very careful to stay near the key while I worked. I was very busy that day but I saw no one go behind the counter. A couple of hours later I discovered the necklace along with the key were gone and that window over there was open." She pointed to a window at the end of the counter.

Alan went to the window and looked out. The window was only about waist high from the outside and someone could have very easily swung his or her legs over the windowsill, crouched down where they wouldn't have been seen, and taken the necklace without Mary knowing.

After talking a few minutes more we promised Mary we would do our very best to locate the missing key. It seemed a lot of people were counting on us.

Chapter Seven

John, Jake, and Billy met us on the edge of town.

"Do you two want to go with us to a spooky spot?" asked Billy.

"A spooky spot?" inquired Alan.

"What kind of spooky spot?" I asked.

"You know, a spooky spot where spooky things can happen," added John.

"Yeah sure, why not?" I added.

"Taylor. We need to be focused on our mission," Alan expressed.

"I know. I know, but we seem to always find out important stuff by exploring. Do you have a better plan?" I asked Alan.

"No." Alan sighed.

As we walked along, John pointed to a small row house and explained that Edgar Alan Poe had once lived there.

"Wow," I exclaimed.

"Cool," said Alan.

The house, really a row house, looked plain, not grand. I guess I thought all famous people lived in huge, grand houses. It rather looked like a house our family had lived in at one time.

We walked on for a ways down the road until we arrived at a graveyard. *Well I guess this could be a spooky spot.*

"Why are we here?" I asked the boys.

John answered, "We want to show you two the catacombs."

Alan and I looked at each other.

"Catacombs?" questioned Alan.

"What catacombs?" I repeated.

"You'll see, follow us," answered Billy.

As we approached the church there was someone waiting in the shadows with a candle glowing

through the dark of night.

"Psst," I made a noise to get Alan's attention.

"What?" Alan asked.

"Do you think we should go there?" I asked. I was feeling the first twinges of uncertainty.

Alan stopped walking. "John, is this place safe?"

John turned. "Sure, it is. We just thought you would like to see it. That's my pa over there with the candle. And Mr. Benson is waiting in the church for us."

"Oh, okay." I said.

The steeple stood tall against the trees. The moon was out tonight, peeking through the passing clouds. I could see the silhouette of the church as we approached. It was a huge building and somewhat intimidating the way it was cast in the shadows.

I knew a lot of history for my age, at least that's what Mom and Dad always said, and I knew this was no longer a church, but, in fact, it was called Westminster Hall now. My second cousin, Reese, had gotten married there four years ago.

We met up with everyone near the entrance to the graveyard. Alan and I were each given a lit candle. We walked into the graveyard and walked directly to the front steps of the gothic looking church; it had a creepy feel. Maybe that was because it was dark, but I was really glad we were with a group of people.

The catacombs were a little spooky but not exactly what I imagined. Actually, my imagination had gotten a little carried away, seeing how I had never really seen catacombs before. I was anticipating a much spookier place.

You know how it is. When you imagine a spooky place, your imagination grows, and becomes a wild beast out of control. I'm an expert in this, daydreaming is my forte. But I daydream responsibly when I am stuck in a car, taking a long trip, or somewhere I am not going anywhere anytime soon.

The door underneath the church led to a dirt interior. It was a few steps down. You could see the huge pillars and there was a musky smell down here, kind of like the air was stale and had been there a very long time. As I walked on I saw the first tomb.

"Alan, is this a graveyard?" I whispered.

"Yeah, but it's called the catacombs," Alan expressed.

"Oh."

In fact, there were a lot of tombs down here. There were separate chambers, for deceased families, along with one big open room for several individuals. In one of the chambers there was a very squeaky, rusty door about waist high. Behind it laid a sort of dirt chute that led to yet another lower portion of the catacombs. When Alan closed it, the eerie sound it made gave me a shiver up my spine. The sound reminded me of a vampire movie where you enter a room that has a vampire in a coffin and he slowly opens it with the same horrible eerie sound.

"Let's get out of here Alan" I urged.

As we were walking by the last area where a single tomb was encased, I felt compelled to have another look before I walked away. I was thinking about what Swing had said, "…the Chest of Treasures is hidden 'by the light of the moon one can see through the shadows; no more, no less, than one pony high.'" There were shadows cast on some of the tombstones by the moonlight in here.

"Alan, wait," I said.

Alan was already moving on, no doubt trying to hurry our tour along.

"What is it Sis?" Alan asked.

"I don't know, but I think we should open that tomb," I said. I pointed to the one on the far wall.

"What? I'm not opening someone's tomb."

"Look," I pointed at the tomb.

The tomb had a grotesque head on it, and the

head seemed to be looking at me.

"So," Alan said. "It has an ogre-like head on the stone, so what?"

The ogre-like head came alive. "Taylor, Alan, you must hurry in your quest to retrieve the key. Newt's tail and spider's eye, the skink knows the way."

And just that fast the grotesque ogre-like head was once again silent. He had delivered a puzzling remark.

"Alan that ogre-like head just gave us a clue I think," I sputtered.

"Yeah, but we have to be careful Taylor," Alan said.

"I know. We have to consider Jalabar and his spies."

"C'mon, let's catch up to the rest of the gang," Alan prodded.

As we walked out I told Alan that I didn't think the ogre-like head worked for Jalabar because I didn't sense anything but a genuine need to help us on his part.

"How would you know if he was being genuine or not?" pointed out Alan.

"I don't really know how I know that, but I do," I persisted.

Alan just shook his head and moved toward the door and the fresh air that waited just beyond the wide wooden door.

Outside in the cool fresh air I did not feel so confined. I didn't think I was claustrophobic but I sure was glad to be outside again. Poe's small head stone lie in the back graveyard in his grandfather's lot.

When they caught up with the group Alan asked Jake, "Do you know where skinks live around here?"

Jake answered, "Skinks live all around, Alan, but there are a whole lot of them down by the creek not far from here."

"Thanks," Alan exclaimed.

Jake gave Alan directions down to the creek. So we planned to go there at first light. The rest of the tour was spooky, just as the boys had promised. Alan and I both loved the rest of the tour just like we loved the haunted house at the ocean-side amusement park. Haunted houses, barns, and the like were really popular during Halloween. Ghosts, people wielding chain saws, clowns, they were all there at the haunted house.

I know this sounds weird, but I think the make-believe houses were scarier than the real houses. I mean the graveyard and hall here were spooky, but I liked being scared at the fake haunted houses more.

Alan and I woke the next morning at Molly's Boarding House and hurried to the spot that Jake had told Alan about. The outcropping of rocks was taller than me. Small and large boulders lay strewn across the area near the creek. Several small rocks near the creek bed had slippery moss on them.

"Do you think we will find a skink here?" I asked Alan.

"I don't know Taylor, but I bet there are a lot of skinks here because they can hide, breed, and they have a good food source all in one location."

"Well, let's spread out," I suggested.

"Okay, sounds good. You go that way and I'll go over there, and we will work our way back to the middle." Alan pointed to the left and indicated I go that way, while he would go toward the right side.

I walked over to the edge of rocks. At first I just walked in front of the outcropping but I couldn't see the whole area very well. I decided to climb on the lower portions of the rocks so that I could peer down in between the rocks. I would go to the other side once I had given this side a good examination.

I wasn't afraid of spiders, and that was a good thing because I saw a lot of spider webs, some going across the rocks, some in between the rocks, but I didn't see one skink anywhere. Taking my time, I looked on both sides of the rocks with no results. All I caught was fleeting glance of one lonely little beetle.

Alan was still methodically looking in each nook and cranny so I just sat down near the creek's edge and looked into the water. There were several small rocks embedded below the water's surface, which made the flowing water shimmer and make sounds as the water flowed over and in between the rocks; just like a babbling brook.

I absentmindedly picked up a rock and tried to make it skip across the water. I had seen Alan and my dad do it several times but no one did it as expertly as my mother. She had explained to Alan and me that her grandfather, Theodore, had taught her many years ago when she was a young girl. Unfortunately, I didn't seem to possess her natural talent.

Alan walked over when he was finished and picked up a rock. He made it skip across the water all the way to the other side. He sat down next to me; "Nothing, not one skink."

"I know. I didn't even see spiders," I added.

"Well what do we do now?" Alan asked.

"I don't know," I answered. I brought my knees toward my chest and hugged them close, resting my chin on top. I pondered what we should do next. I glanced over at Alan and saw he was concentrating as well.

"Maybe we are looking a little too hard," Alan said. "Maybe we need to sit quietly and wait to see what happens. Obviously, we are scaring the wildlife with all our loud noises."

Okay, maybe he had a point. I knew wildlife as a general rule tried to stay away from us humans with good cause I might add. I had recently heard two teachers talking in the hallway about the newest statistic that half of the world's wildlife population had been lost in just the last four decades. That is so, so sad. I really hope we can change our ways, be more responsible, and help turn our world into a better place.

We sat there perfectly quiet for a long time, perhaps more than twenty minutes. Little by little we saw creatures venture out of their hiding spots. Beetles, creepy crawly thingies, and several bird species, came to the water's edge. I nudged Alan's elbow, he followed my eyes as a herd of deer approached the far end of the creek. The buck's watchful eyes saw us but chose to bring the herd to drink anyway.

Then we saw a groundhog and a small possum arrive as well.

"Alan, psst...look, over there," I whispered.

A skink, no bigger than the palm of my hand was carefully making his way out of the rocks moving cautiously toward the creek. His head was slender like the rest of his body, with a dark brown line from his head to his tail. Although he was mainly beige, you could see the tail was somewhat iridescent blue, a really cute little fellow. I wondered how a skink was supposed to help us find the key.

We watched him quietly. We made no movements whatsoever—just waited. I can sit quietly for long stretches, but when I *know* that I am not supposed to move, I find it most difficult to stay still. I suddenly felt a spot on my head I had the urge to scratch. I needed to shift my pants a little, and my nose was itchy. Oh no, I think I need to...sneeze! I desperately tried to hold it in, but that wasn't going to work this time. I felt a massive sneeze emerging... ah choo!!

This was no small sneeze and it sent the wildlife running in all directions. Darn it. I had really tried not to sneeze, and Alan understood this when he looked into my eyes.

We both saw the skink run, not to the nearest line of rocks, but to an opening farther down. *Maybe our luck has changed.*

Quickly making our way to where the skink ran, we could see a small hole between the rocks.

"Well he's gone," stated Alan. "We might as well leave. He won't be coming back out for a while."

Alan sat up and walked over to pick up another rock to skip across the water. This time it made several skips until it landed on the other side.

I bent down to peer inside the hole to see if I could see anything. Nothing. I put my ear to the hole and tried listening. I thought I heard a faint sound like singing. What could this be I wondered to myself, and then it dawned on me it just might be the key.

"Alan, Alan, come here! I think I can hear singing."

Alan ran back over. I sat up and let him try.

"Taylor, I hear it. I hear it."

One of us had to put our arm down there and feel around for the key. I didn't want to stick my arm in there. What if a snake lived in there—a huge snake? What if a badger lived in there and currently was looking for food? What if creepy crawly thingies were asleep in there and would crawl all over me and poop on me. Yuck. No, no way would this girl put her hand down there.

Alan looked at me. He bravely stuck his arm midway down the hole. The opening between the rocks was very small, very narrow.

"Taylor, I can't get my arm to go any further. My arm is too big. You will have to try."

My stomach was dancing around in my throat. Alan and I both could hear singing now. It must be the key. I hope it's the key.

"C'mon Taylor, I can't do it but you can," encouraged Alan.

"Okay, okay already, I'll try."

I took a deep breath and forced my arm and my mind to go down as far as it would take to retrieve the key. I could feel the coolness of the soil on my arm. Something, I'm pretty sure it was creepy crawly, skimmed across my knuckles. I made my mind blank, so I wouldn't be so scared and plunged farther.

The singing was becoming louder and louder, a sweet melody, something familiar.

I felt something. It was small, cool to the touch, and had jagged ends. The singing was much louder now. I put my fingers around the object and pulled it carefully out of the hole. The tingling sensation increased and it felt like the key was vibrating.

"Look," I said. I held up the key. The key was dirty so I wiped it off with my jeans. It had a really old design to it; swirls and a very unusual pattern that caught my eye. "It must be a one of a kind Alan."

"Yeah. We have to be really careful with it."

Chapter Eight

We both heard a whooshing sound, like the branches and leaves were being pushed aside.

"Hello Taylor, Alan." A man dressed in a full length robe appeared near the clearing. The cape or robe, whatever it was, covered his arms and legs and was a deep, dark purple. He had a hat, a pointy hat on.

I immediately stuffed the key into my jeans pocket and scooted back against the rocks.

He looked at the sign of worry in my eyes and smiled. "Hello," he said again.

Alan demanded, "Who are you and how do you know us?"

"Now children, let's not play games. You know I am Jalabar and I have come for the key. My inept assistant lost the key once he had retrieved it. Lost it right near here, fell asleep only to wake and find the key missing. I knew you would lead me right to it. All I had to do was patiently wait."

He held his hand out. "Please give it to me or else you won't like what I can and will do next."

Alan stood up in front of me. "You cannot have it Jalabar—no way."

Jalabar mumbled several words, words that didn't make any sense to me. I could feel the key moving in my pocket, trying to make its way out. I pushed my hand down as hard as I could to prevent it from exiting but it was coming out. I decided to grab the key with my fingers and hold on. As soon as I physically touched the key it stopped moving.

Jalabar looked angry. "Give me that key!"

"No." I screamed and stood up.

I didn't have any idea what we should do next, but I knew we couldn't give him the key. Alan was concentrating again I could tell by the way he was standing. But what could we do against the power of Jalabar?

Jalabar's hand flung an unseen force my way. I raised my hands, palms out, and screamed, "No!"

Whatever it was it didn't harm Alan or me. Jalabar just stared at me in astonishment. He weaved his hands in a pattern and opened a deep hole in front of us. Alan grabbed my arm and ran in the opposite direction. We didn't get very far before we stopped in our tracks.

I couldn't see anything in front of us but yet I couldn't go forward anymore. When I tried moving to the left or right the same thing happened. We couldn't move forward. I kept my fingers around the key. I looked to Alan.

He was looking behind Jalabar where our three friends were now standing. John had a big burlap bag in his hands. He opened it and motioned to Alan.

Alan said, "Jalabar you are a very weak wizard. Taylor and I will easily defeat you. You will never get the key from us."

Alan made his best attempt to distract Jalabar. A second too late Jalabar heard something and started to turn. John raised the burlap bag and brought it down over Jalabar's head.

John tackled him to the ground. "Run!" He screamed as he scrambled to get up and run as well.

We were all running together to get behind the rocks.

"Are you alright?" Alan asked me.

"Yeah I think so. How about you?"

"I'm okay."

"Thanks you guys," Alan expressed. "Perfect timing."

We all knew Jalabar would be free any minute now.

Alan said, "Call Bella. Call Bella."

Immediately Bella appeared. "Oh dear, I was afraid this would happen."

She walked over to Jalabar. "Jalabar you mustn't harm these children, I forbid it."

She raised her voice, and began to weave a pattern with her hands, when Jalabar quickly said a string of words that stopped Bella from being heard.

We could all see she was talking but it was like her volume had been turned to mute.

Jalabar looked to us kids. "Bella is now my captive, if you want to save Bella, give me the key now."

I knew we couldn't give him the key but what could we do?

Alan said, "I think we have to give him the key."

"No, Alan we can't. Then all will be lost."

"You're right," Alan quickly agreed. We have to find the Chest of Treasures. If we have the Chest of Treasures, Jalabar will give us Bella," Alan stated.

We snuck behind the rocks and trees and headed back the way we came. Right before we were out of sight I stood behind a stand of trees and tried to see what Jalabar was doing. He just stood there looking at our retreating backs.

"Alan I think I know where the Chest of Treasures might be!" I told Alan.

"Where?"

"I think it might be in the catacombs."

"Yeah, that's what I think too," Alan added.

We quickened our pace and reached the catacombs in no time. Jake and John elected to watch over the entrance for any sign of Jalabar. Billy, Alan, and I crept into the dark shadows.

The catacombs looked much different this time round. The gloomy atmosphere was enough to send you running from the place but we needed to be brave. Bella and the Land of Baltimore needed our help.

John called to us, "I found a candle you can use."

Alan came back with a lit candle. That was a relief. We walked in front of the ogre-like head on the cast-iron tomb door. He tried the handle but it wouldn't budge.

The ogre-like head blinked his eyes and spoke, "Three questions first before you enter."

Billy jumped back, clearly frightened by a talking ogre-like head on a tomb.

"It's okay Billy, he has talked to us before."

The ogre-like head continued, "What year did Baltimore fight in the War of 1812?"

"That's easy," I said. I was about to say 1812 but stopped myself. It was a trick question because Baltimore had actually fought in 1814 in the War of 1812.

I elbowed Alan. "I got this."

"Baltimore fought in 1814 in the War of 1812," I answered crossing my fingers I was right.

"You are correct." The ogre-like head merely continued. "Frances Scott Key gave us the National Anthem, this is true, but whose artistic hand has sewn the enormous flag that flew overhead during the battle?"

Alan and Billy looked questioningly at me. I had a book back home all about her, the woman who tirelessly worked on the flag. If only I could remember her name. I tapped my foot trying to shake my memory. Then it came to me.

"Mary Pickersgill," I proudly announced.

"You are correct." The ogre-like head showed no expression. "Name one poem or short story that Edgar Allan Poe wrote?"

Alan whispered, "I know this one." Then he turned and said, "The Raven."

The ogre-like head stated, "You are correct."

The ogre-like head was again silent. Alan opened the tomb and we all saw the Chest of Treasures. It was a chest much like one I imagine a pirate would hide his booty in; it was an old antique wooden chest. The lid was intricately carved with swirls on top. The keyhole caught my attention. I carefully brought the key out of my pocket.

I looked at Alan and he nodded, silently urging me to proceed. I put the key in the Chest of Treasures while Alan held my hand for support. My hand was shaking so hard that my first attempt failed. I tried again holding the key more firmly.

I felt a slight shift as the key turned in the key-hole but I was afraid to open the lid. What if a terrible power was unleashed and we were unable to stop it? What if a genie popped out? But I guess genies are only in bottles. Well, what if we opened the lid and we were trapped inside the tomb forever? I was let-ting my imagination get the better of me.

I stood back. "I think you should open it Alan, I don't think I can."

"Okay." Alan carefully, slowly, opened the lid. There was no noise. I expected to hear a squeaking sound, something, but the silence was drawn out and scarier than anything I have ever experienced before.

I was about to grab Alan and plead for him not to open it when he opened it fully. I stood staring at it. Alan stared at it. The *contents* were frighteningly empty.

Billy looked at Taylor and Alan's expression when the Chest of Treasures was opened. There were no treasures that he could see but he did see an arch of light that seemed to come from the Chest of Treasures and surround both Alan and Taylor. Just as fast the image, that looked something like a see-thru flame, was gone. He stood there thinking about what it might mean.

Alan put his hand inside just to make sure nothing was there that was invisible. The Chest of Treasures was empty. He slowly closed the lid and brought it out of the tomb.

"Maybe someone else got here first?" Alan suggested.

"Maybe, but I don't think so," I said.

Alan closed the tomb door. Instantly, the ogre-like head spoke again.

"Sprinkle some dirt from the catacomb's floor on Jalabar while reciting this phrase, 'Not once but

twice the staying power, hold hands and feet, move not but cower.'"

The ogre-like head fell silent. His face maintained a cold stone look.

I put a handful of dirt from the floor inside my front pocket of my jeans. We met the boys outside and hurried back to the spot where Jalabar had captured Bella.

Jalabar was standing there with a smug look on his face. Confident he would get the key along with the Chest of Treasures, and the Land of Baltimore would be helpless against his new power, he was no doubt planning his take over.

Alan spoke to Jalabar who was waiting with Bella. Bella stood stark still unable to move or speak.

"We have the Chest of Treasures and the key, now let Bella go!"

Jalabar responded, "I care not for Bella, you can have her. Give me the Chest of Treasures and the key," he gestured with his hands.

Alan laid the Chest of Treasures down on a nearby rock. He said, "You can only have the key when Bella is let loose from your hold on her."

"So be it," Jalabar stated.

Bella immediately sagged down until she caught herself from falling. She walked quickly over toward us kids.

"Now give me the key or you will feel the wrath of Jalabar."

I took the key out of my pocket and laid it down on the ground.

"No—bring the key to me, quickly," Jalabar again gestured with his hands. He looked very agitated.

I picked it up and moved closer to the Chest of Treasures and placed the key next to it. I backed up several steps. Jalabar quickly ran over and grabbed the key. He inserted the key into the keyhole.

I saw my chance and took it. I removed the dirt from my pocket and flung it toward Jalabar. I recited the phrase, "Not once but twice the staying power, hold hands and feet, move not but cower." I mumbled it beneath my breath so Jalabar couldn't understand my words but I had been too anxious, too clumsy. The dirt didn't land on any part of Jalabar. Nothing happened.

Oh no, I didn't have any more dirt. Jalabar would rule the land. I had let down Bella, let down Alan; I had let down the good people of the Land of Baltimore.

I looked for Alan and found him sneaking up behind Jalabar. He had his hand in his pocket. By this time Jalabar had turned the key and was opening the lid of the Chest of Treasures.

Before he could open it fully Alan yelled, "Say it again Taylor—loud and clear."

I understood. I repeated, "Not once but twice the staying power, hold hands and feet, move not but cower."

Alan threw a handful of the dirt from the catacombs on Jalabar's back.

Jalabar fell to the ground, holding both his hands and feet. He tried moving, wiggling even, but could not let go of his limbs. It looked like the stretches we did for warm-ups before our yoga class began. Funny.

He was infuriated. His pointy hat was askew, falling over his brow such that he could only see with one eye. "I will get revenge, mark my words," he bellowed.

Bella waved her hands and Jalabar was silent but his brooding eyes looked like he wanted to throw daggers at us.

Bella hugged us in turn. She was beaming with joy. Bella said she would take Jalabar away and would meet up with us later in town. We were all exhausted and didn't argue. I was feeling quite proud that we were able to defeat Jalabar. I was also beginning to miss home.

Chapter Nine

After much discussion about how things had turned out and how it would impact the Land of Baltimore forever more, we just enjoyed a few minutes of peace. I watched the babbling water as it meandered over the rocks rushing to meet the bay.

A little later in the day Bella met us near Mary's Kitchen Corner. She motioned for us to join her. The boys hastily said their goodbyes but Bella called out for all of us to join her.

Several tables were put side by side to accommodate our crowd. Alan and I sat directly across from Bella.

"I don't get it? The Chest of Treasures was empty," I said while looking at Bella.

Bella answered, "Not quite. Zanzar was a very powerful wizard centuries ago." She didn't elaborate, she just smiled.

Alan started to talk but Bella continued, "The Chest of Treasures is now safe from the likes of Jalabar. I thank you all."

She looked around the table slowly, smiling and nodding her head as her eyes met each person. "You have all conducted yourselves bravely this day. I am most proud."

Then she looked at Alan and I. "We will need a new protector, a new keeper of the key. Who shall it be?"

Leaning in, Alan and I spoke quietly together.

I raised my head and said, "Alan and I feel strongly that Billy should be the new keeper of the key."

Billy just shook his head, like he didn't believe we had said his name. "Me? Did you just say me?" Billy questioned. He looked around at everyone seated.

"A fine choice," Bella agreed.

Billy stuttered, "I…I can't be. I can't be the

keeper of the key. Don't you remember my story I done told you?" He looked to Alan and me. "You don't want me. I won't make a good keeper of the key."

Bella raised her hand for quiet. "You will make a fine keeper of the key indeed." She placed the key that was attached to a long necklace around his neck. "From this day forward, you along with your family will protect at all costs this key given into your care, till the end of time."

Billy looked like he might cry. "Thank you," he said quietly.

Bella called to Mary, "We are ready for today's special."

Our meals were delicious. I savored each morsel, taking as long as I could. I didn't want to have to say goodbye but I knew it was time. I felt sad and happy at the same time, if that was possible. I really didn't want to leave the Land of Baltimore but I really missed Mom and Dad. I think Alan felt the same. We both had made friends we would never forget.

"Psst…Alan. Let's give this to the boys to share." I pointed to my new portable checkers set that hung from my neck to my waist. It was a cool knapsack and I had seen all the boys eyeing it.

"Great idea."

"John, Jake, Billy" I said emphatically, "Alan and I want to leave you something to remember us by. Please take this knapsack, it's a portable checkers set and you will have fun playing with it."

Each boy thanked us. I was getting a little teary-eyed.

"It's time," Bella said gently. She must have known how we were feeling because she said, "I will forever be grateful for your help Taylor and Alan. I hope to see you again sometime soon but I also know your parents will miss you if you do not leave and return home."

The boys said their goodbyes again and hugged us. We walked down the street to the train station waving to John, Jake, and Billy as we went.

As we boarded the train for the return trip, I turned and waved to Bella who was standing on the platform. I liked her a lot; she was a really good wizard I thought. We sat in our seats and looked out the window. Bella was trying to say something but I don't know how to read lips that well unless it was my mom's, which I was pretty used to.

All I had to do was look at my mother and I could read a lot of what she was saying. Like, T-a-y-l-o-r, drawn out with each syllable enunciated. Or, if she was talking to Alan and she said "No. I said Nooo!" I didn't need to be able to hear those words; all I had to do was read my mother's lips. Anyway, Alan reached over and opened the window so we could better hear her.

"You know your great-grandfather, Nathan, would be proud. You both make a fine pair of ..."

I couldn't hear the last word she said. The train whistle blew and the train slowly pulled away from the station. The train strained against the weight and jerked until it gained momentum.

"What?" I yelled out the window. "What did you just say?"

Bella responded, she appeared to be repeating herself but I still couldn't hear her. "Did you hear what she said?" I questioned Alan.

"No. I'm not sure what she said either. A fine pair of …what I wonder?" Alan questioned mostly to himself.

Chapter Ten

We had already begun our journey home and as we rounded the bend I got my last glimpse of Bella. I settled down into my seat pondering what she had said. Well, we sure did have a wonderful time on this adventure, I thought to myself. Yes, this adventure business was exciting stuff I decided. Helping people felt really good—and I knew it was the right thing to do. I hugged myself.

"What?" Alan asked as he looked at me.

"Oh, I'm just really happy we helped out. It feels right to be helping, Alan. I like it."

"Me too, Taylor."

"I mean I know some of it is dangerous but we are making a difference Alan. I never knew I could do that."

"Sure you did. You make a difference everyday Taylor. You do good work in school, you help Mom and Dad out all the time, and you are a very good sister and Girl Scout."

I was on the verge of tears. "Thanks Alan. You are the very best brother ever." I loved my brother even though sometimes he bugged me.

We sat in silence for the rest of the train ride, lost in our own thoughts. When we disembarked from the train, Alan started looking around for where we were supposed to go next.

All Bella had told us was, "Walk the path from the train station and when you see a fork in the road go left, keep walking until you see something unusual." That was all she had said. What that meant exactly neither of us knew.

As we walked down the path I was already beginning to feel anxious to get back home. My family, my friends, I suddenly missed them all.

Alan nudged me with his elbow, "Taylor—look."

I looked up and saw a unicorn standing in the middle of the path. After a moment of stunned realization that a real live, unicorn was right in front of us, I was the happiest girl alive.

"Well, she certainly is unusual," I said to Alan.

"She certainly is," replied Alan.

We walked forward. The unicorn whinnied softly and brought her front leg down.

"I guess she wants us to climb up. I think we are going for a ride," stated Alan.

"Let's go," I said excitedly. *I'm going to ride a unicorn. Correction, a magnificent unicorn. How cool is that?*

She was all white with strikingly beautiful green eyes. She let us pet her; her mane was soft and smooth to the touch. Alan still had an apple in his pocket from the outdoor café and he offered it to the unicorn. She graciously accepted it and whinnied some more.

She set out at a somewhat slow pace and then began to trot faster as she understood we could hold on. I was enjoying myself. The wind blew my hair in my face but I didn't want to let go of Alan's back. I had my arms wrapped around his waist and he was bent over holding onto the unicorn's neck. This was the most exhilarating ride of my life. I was riding a unicorn. I, Taylor, was riding a unicorn.

The unicorn came to a halt in front of a huge boulder. She lowered her leg so we could better get down. I shimmied down the unicorn's back and then helped Alan down. I hugged the unicorn goodbye.

As we were leaving, something made me turn around. The unicorn was just standing there looking at us.

"In your future travels, beware of Tarina." Then she trotted swiftly away. She was out of sight within a few seconds. Not enough time for me to even close my hanging, wide-open mouth.

"Did you hear what the unicorn just said?" I asked Alan.

"Yeah. It was pretty cool," answered Alan. "I wonder who Tarina is."

"Maybe a what, not who," stated Taylor.

"She said 'future travels,' stated Alan. "What does *that* mean?"

"It means...," stated Taylor "That you and I will be doing this again."

We walked a short distance. I was still thinking about a talking unicorn, and why I didn't think to ask her some questions, when we rounded the corner. Just as I knew we would, we saw a cave. Well, what I meant to say was that I knew we would see something out of the ordinary, when we went around the bend.

Nothing plain and drab, or ordinary for Alan and me; no, it seemed we were destined for exciting drama in different lands. Why, I mused? Why us? I'm just a kid in elementary school. And, a really good Girl Scout, I corrected.

The cave entrance was really just a small opening about five feet across and four feet high. Neither of us needed to ask the other if this was the right place to enter. We knew, I'm not sure how we knew, but we knew. I think I was beginning to understand we somehow belonged here. A part of me really liked our new found adventures.

As we walked, I could feel a strong breeze pushing me forward, like I was being sucked into the cave's mouth; it was a bizarre feeling. I should have felt something more along the lines of screaming out of fright, but I wasn't the least bit afraid. Not really; a little apprehensive maybe—but not scared. Maybe I should be scared. I heard a roaring sound, a little like a freight train racing down the tracks.

Alan looked over at me. “Hold my hand, Taylor. Now.”

He took hold of my hand just before…”

Chapter Eleven

In an instant we were back in the theater with all the goodies in our hands. The drinks were still cold and the popcorn was filled to the top of the box with melted butter drizzled on top.

"Cool," said Alan as he looked down.

"Yeah, cool," I added. I looked around and saw the backs of the new, plush seats in the theater. I could smell that new smell. I saw the cup holders with the pull-out trays. Those plastic conveniences never looked so good.

I felt for my necklace that I always wore. The one Nadia had given to me. Alan had one too. It was made out of some kind of shiny metal. It hung from a tiny chain; the flat medallion was rhombus-shaped with a series of symbols on it.

We quickly walked to theater number eight and saw Mom and Dad. We hurried over to our seats.

"What took you so long? The movie is about to begin," exclaimed Mom. "Was there a very long line at the concession stand Alan?" inquired Mom.

"Yes. A boy spilled his soda and then stepped on Taylor's toes," Alan commented.

"Are you okay Taylor? Mom asked. She had that concerned motherly look on her face. I decided right then that I loved that concerned look she got on her face, where before it sometimes annoyed me.

"I'm fine—just fine." And I meant it. I looked over at Alan and winked. I then settled back into my comfy seat.

"Okay hush," said Dad. "The movie is starting."

Even Dad wanted to the see, "The Mushroom Had a Top." And *that* was my trip to see the very best movie ever.

Notes

Edith Houghton Hooker worked to help women gain the right to vote. She lived in Baltimore, Maryland. She formed a group called the Just Government League which was a part of the National American Woman Suffrage Association (NAWSA). The NAWSA was a merger of the National Woman Suffrage Association (NWSA) and the American Woman Suffrage Association (AWSA). Before the 19th amendment was passed on August 18, 1920 women in the United States of America could not vote. Today, with their primary goal already achieved, the group is now called the League of Women Voters.

Born in 1872, William Henry Keeler, or Wee Willie, was a real player for the Baltimore Orioles. He helped his team win the 1894 National Pennant. The game was actually played against the Cleveland Spider's in Cleveland. It is said that when the Orioles won the game, they were cheered and congratulated all the way back to their hotel. Mr. Keeler was widely known for the "Baltimore Chop." Wee Willie died in 1923 and was later inducted into the Hall of Fame in 1939.

Juliette Low was the founder of Girl Scouts. Her passions included art and helping young girls. Born in Savannah, Georgia, Juliette Magill Kinzie Gordon Low, was given the nickname Daisy, which she was called her entire life. Using her own funds she formed Girl Scouts of the United States of America (GSUSA) in 1912.

Today, the Girl Scouts have close to 6 million members and is the largest educational organization for girls in the world.

Cannery Row - Where Baltimore canned goods from the early 1800s to the early 1900s. Baltimore was the first city to can oysters because the Chesapeake oysters were so plentiful. Vital sources of protein, oysters were very popular. At one time Baltimore harvested 14 million bushels annually. But over harvesting and environmental causes have led to drastic reductions.

Francis Scott Key penned the poem, "Defence of Fort McHenry," that later became the U.S. National Anthem, while in the Baltimore Harbor during the War of 1812. The attack on Ft. McHenry began on September 13th for more than 27 hours.

Mary Pickersgill was commissioned by Major George Armistead to make a flag for Ft. McHenry. She and her 13 year old daughter made the flag that was flown overhead during the battle. Later, Mary was involved in many social issues, including being president of the Impartial Female Humane

Society. She is buried in southwest Baltimore. Her daughter erected a monument for her. Her home, the Star-Spangled Banner Flag House, is located in Baltimore.

Edgar Allan Poe was born in 1809 and died in 1849. He wrote mostly poetry and short stories. Some of his most famous works are called the Raven, and The Fall of the House of Usher. He is considered the first person to write in the detective fiction genre, along with the emerging science fiction genre, as well as trying to earn a living on his writing alone. Dying under mysterious circumstances, he is buried beside his wife and aunt in Baltimore's Westminster Burial Grounds.

You can find out more about these interesting places and people, and get all the facts at your local library.

Glossary

Apprehensive – Having anxiety or alarm about the future.

Approximately – It is almost exact, almost correct but is not precise.

Blacksmith – A person who makes or repairs horse-shoes and other things made out of iron.

Catacombs – An underground cemetery with recesses for the tombs.

Claustrophobic – Not enough space to feel comfortable.

Commotion – A loud or noisy confusion.

Conveniences – Something you may use that enables you to do things more easily.

Crucial – Very important or significant.

Decade – Each decade is ten years.

Elaborate – To give much detail.

Enunciated – To pronounce each word or parts of words clearly.

Galaxy – A very large group of stars.

Humongous – To be extremely large or huge.

Inept – Unable to perform her/his skill well.

Interjected – Interrupt with a remark, perhaps to change the subject.

Intrigued – The mystery, the lure, or the making of secret plans.

Invaders – Persons who plunder or conquest.

Livery stable – Place where horses are housed, kept short-term or rented out.

Masquerade – A social gathering of where you wear masks and/or costumes.

Methodically – Usually done in a very careful, organized way.

Momentum – The force that grows stronger or faster as time passes by.

Oblivious – Lacking an awareness.

Ogre – Something or perhaps someone who is very frightening.

Patrons – One who uses services or buys goods.

Rationalize – To describe something in a way that will explain it so it seems more attractive.

Rebellion – Refusal to obey the rules; opposition to one in authority.

Rhombus – A shape that has four sides, equal in length with four angles, but does always have right angles.

Scrumptious – Delicious, excellent.

Skink – A common lizard. It grows up to 8 inches long with five light stripes down their backs.

Statistic – A number representing a piece of information.

Suspenders – A fashion accessory; generally used to hold up pants.

Tack – An accessory used with horses. Such as: bridles, saddles, stirrups, bits, etc.

Jackie Mae and Alison Taylor

Please consider giving this book a review. If you liked it that would be great, but good or bad we would just love your opinion. Writers live and die by their reviews. You have the power to help this book succeed. Thank you in advance. May health and happiness be in abundance always surrounding you.

Please look for the next Taylor and Alan Adventure coming soon.

Please connect with Jackie Mae at:

jackiemaebooks@gmail.com

http://www.facebook.com/AuthorJackieMae

http://www.twitter.com/JackieMacAuthor

Please visit Jackie's blog:

http://www.jackiemae-author.blogspot.com

Please visit Jackie's website:

http://www.jackiemae.com

Made in the USA
Middletown, DE
14 February 2015